The Magic School Bus
Inside a Beehive

By Joanna Cole / Illustrated by Bruce Degen

Scholastic Inc.
New York · Toronto · London · Auckland · Sydney
Mexico City · New Delhi · Hong Kong · Buenos Aires

The author and illustrator wish to thank Professor Mark L. Winston, Department of Biological Sciences,
Simon Fraser University, British Columbia, Canada, for his assistance in preparing this book.

For their helpful advice and consultation, thanks also to Ray Pupedis,
Division of Entomology, Yale-Peabody Museum of Natural History, New Haven, Connecticut;
Eric H. Erickson, Center Director, Carl Hayden Bee Research Center, Tuscon, Arizona;
and Mark Richardson, who kindly gave us a tour of his beehive.

ISBN-13: 978-0-590-25721-3
ISBN-10: 0-590-25721-8

32   10 11/0

Printed in the U.S.A.   40

The illustrator used pen and ink, watercolor, color pencil,
and gouache for the paintings in this book.

To my
honey, Phil.

J.C.

To
Will Tressler
and Jim Setz, and
all the busy bees who
are building our new hive.

B.D.

"What a perfect spring day!"
said Ms. Frizzle, looking out the window.
We thought it was perfect, too —
perfect for playing softball.
But the Friz had something else in mind.
"It's just right for observing honey bees!"

BEE OBSERVANT
LOOK CLOSELY AT INSECTS

INSECT CHECKLIST

ALL ADULT INSECTS:

ALWAYS HAVE 6 LEGS

ALWAYS HAVE 3 BODY SECTIONS

USUALLY HAVE WINGS

USUALLY HAVE ANTENNAE

HEAD
THORAX
ABDOMEN

Fly

Honey bees are insects. Here are some other insects.

THERE ARE MORE INSECT SPECIES ON EARTH THAN ALL OTHER ANIMALS PUT TOGETHER!

YES, BUT DO THEY ALL HAVE TO BE IN OUR CLASSROOM?

IS A SPIDER AN INSECT?

No! SPIDERS HAVE EIGHT LEGS AND TWO BODY SECTIONS

SPIDERS ARE RELATIVES OF INSECTS

DOROTHY ANN'S BIG BOOK OF BEES

LUNCH

Wasp

Cockroach

Ant

Housefly

6

We had been studying about all different kinds of insects.
Now Ms. Frizzle said she had found a beekeeper who would show us his honey bee hives.

SOME KINDS OF BEES
by Florrie
There are more than 20,000 different kinds of bees.
Here are some of them:

HONEY BEE →
BUMBLE BEE
CARPENTER BEE →
ORCHID BEE

UH-OH!

BUZZ!
QUIT BUGGING ME!

Cricket   Dragonfly   Goliath Beetle   Mosquito

As we boarded the old school bus, Ms. Frizzle talked and talked about honey bees. "They make a delicious food for us to eat," she said. "They help many plants survive. *And* they are wonderful examples of social insects!"

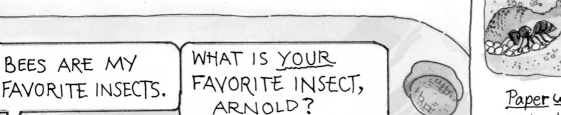

BEES ARE MY FAVORITE INSECTS.

WHAT IS YOUR FAVORITE INSECT, ARNOLD?

...I'M NOT THE KIND OF PERSON WHO HAS A FAVORITE INSECT.

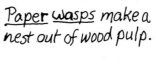

Ants nest in the ground.

Paper wasps make a nest out of wood pulp.

Bumble bees nest in grass-lined holes in the ground.

Termites nest in wood.

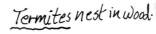

A WORD FROM DOROTHY ANN
Social comes from a word that means "friend" or "partner."

9

WHY DO BEES STING?
by Phoebe

Stinging is the way bees protect their hive. Bees usually sting only if they have to. That's because they die soon after they sting.

> I'LL STING, BUT ONLY FOR A GOOD CAUSE...

> ...SUCH AS SAVING THE HIVE.

Honey bees have barbs, or hooks, on the end of their stingers.

STINGER   BARB

When a honey bee stings, her stinger gets stuck in the victim's skin. The stinger is pulled out of the bee's body, and the bee **dies**.

Ms. Frizzle drove out into the country and parked the bus next to the hives. The beekeeper was late, so Frizzie took out a picnic basket. "Some light refreshments will pass the time while we wait," she said. Sometimes, our teacher has *good* ideas!

BEE AROUND STINGING INSECTS CAREFU

> BEES USUALLY WILL NOT STING, UNLESS YOU TOUCH THEM, ANNOY THEM, OR GET TOO CLOSE TO THEIR HIVE.

> MAY WE CLOSE THE WINDOWS, PLEASE?

HONEY

But just as she opened
a jar of honey,
her elbow knocked
a strange little lever.
The honey jar fell, and
we heard a weird
buzzing sound.

It was the bus.
It was vibrating,
and getting smaller.
So was everything in it —
including *us*!

ALLERGIC TO BEE STINGS
by Ralphie
Some people get very sick
and can even die from
bee stings.
They have to carry
special medicine.

One by one, we stepped out the door and looked over at the nearest hive. At the entrance, worker bees were standing guard. "Guard bees usually keep out bees from other hives," said the Friz.

ENTRANCE

GUARD BEE IN POSITION TO MEET INCOMING BEES

ACCORDING TO MY RESEARCH, GUARD BEES WILL BITE AND STING STRANGE BEES.

DO WE QUALIFY AS "STRANGE BEES"?

NO DOUBT ABOUT IT!

DOROTHY ANN'S BIG BOOK OF BEES

13

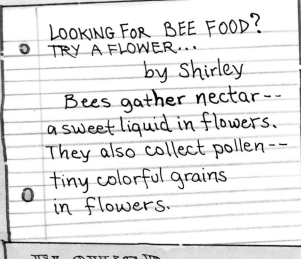

LOOKING FOR BEE FOOD?
TRY A FLOWER...
　　　　by Shirley

Bees gather nectar --
a sweet liquid in flowers.
They also collect pollen --
tiny colorful grains
in flowers.

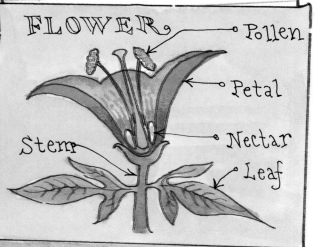

FLOWER

Pollen

Petal

Nectar

Leaf

Stem

"There is *one* time when guard bees
may let in a strange bee," said Ms. Frizzle.
"Sometimes a hive may 'adopt' a lost bee —
if it is carrying a lot of bee food.
All bee food comes from flowers.

BEES EAT ONLY NECTAR AND POLLEN,
AND FOODS THEY <u>MAKE</u> FROM
NECTAR AND POLLEN.

WHAT? NO CHIPS?

THE AVERAGE BEE
VISITS THOUSANDS
OF FLOWERS
EVERY DAY.

NOW I KNOW WHY
THEY CALL THEM
<u>BUSY</u> BEES !

"We'll have to visit flowers and get bee food in order to gain entrance to the hive. Follow that bee!" shouted the Friz. We flew after a bee that was headed toward some bright flowers.

MEANWHILE

COMING FROM THE EAST

EXACTLY WHAT DOES SHE MEAN BY "GAIN ENTRANCE TO THE HIVE"?

SHE MEANS GO INSIDE IT.

I WAS AFRAID OF THAT...

FLYING IS FUN!

BUZZ OFF!

15

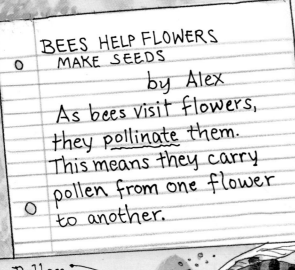

BEES HELP FLOWERS
MAKE SEEDS
by Alex

As bees visit flowers, they pollinate them. This means they carry pollen from one flower to another.

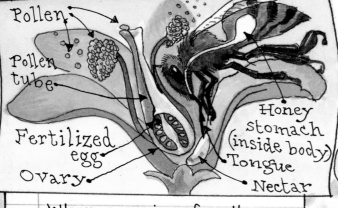

Pollen

Pollen tube

Fertilized egg

Ovary

Honey stomach (inside body)

Tongue

Nectar

When a grain of pollen joins with an egg cell in a flower, a seed begins to grow.

MANY PLANTS CANNOT MAKE SEEDS UNLESS BEES POLLINATE THEIR FLOWERS.

WE NEED BEES!

"Observe our bee, children,
and do exactly what she does!"
Ms. Frizzle called.
The bee stuck her long tubelike tongue
deep into a flower and pumped out nectar.
We each did the same with a rubber tube.
"The bee carries the nectar in a pouch
called the honey stomach," Frizzie told us.
We carried our nectar in a tiny bottle.

BEE POLLINATE THEM! KIND TO FLOWERS

BE A BEE! COLLECT NECTAR AND POLLEN.

16

Pollen grains rubbed off the flower
and stuck onto the bee's "fur."
With her front and middle legs,
she combed off the pollen and packed it
into pollen baskets —
pouches on her back legs.
Then she returned to the hive.
We packed our pollen and went along.

BEES HELP MAKE FOOD FOR PEOPLE
by John
Bees pollinate many **crop** plants -- plants **that** give us our food.

Apple

Blueberry

Squash

Orange

POLLEN BASKET

AT MY OLD SCHOOL, WE NEVER COLLECTED FLOWER PRODUCTS.

IF WE HAVE A LOT, MAYBE THE BEES WON'T STING US.

I'M GETTING EXTRA!

POLLEN BASKET

WE NEED BEES!

17

BEES "TALK" WITH SMELLS!
by Amanda Jane

PHEROMONES are body chemicals that allow animals to "talk" to each other by smell.

With pheromones, bees send each other many messages. Here are some of them:
"I'm a hive-mate."
"I'm a stranger."
"I'm a worker."
"I'm the queen bee!"
"Danger! Danger!"
"Defend the hive!"

Bees don't talk in words, but they do communicate.

One by one, we landed at the hive.
The Friz sprayed us with a bee pheromone —
a chemical that bees make.
Now we smelled like bees.
Then came the scary part.

We held our breath as the guard bees brushed us with their antennae, smelling us. If they fell for our trick, we'd get into the hive. If they didn't, we'd get into big trouble!

WE'RE TAKING A BIG CHANCE.

I'LL BUZZ TO THAT!

WORK ORDERS

☑ Guard entrance
☑ Clean hive
☑ Build comb
☑ Make honey
☑ Fan wings to cool hive
☑ Tend queen
☑ Feed baby bees
☑ Collect pollen and nectar

WHO'S WHO IN THE HIVE?
by Michael

In a honey bee colony, there are three castes, or kinds, of bees:

1. The <u>QUEEN</u>: Her job is to lay eggs, eggs, and more eggs!

QUEEN

2. The <u>WORKERS</u>: They are all female bees that usually do not lay eggs. Workers do almost all the jobs in the hive.

3. The <u>DRONES</u> are all male bees. A male bee's only job is to mate with a queen.

WORKER   DRONE

19

A BEEHIVE COMES IN SECTIONS
by Molly

TOP

INSIDE COVER

"SUPER" FRAMES (HOLD THE EXTRA HONEY WE TAKE TO EAT)

QUEEN EXCLUDER (KEEPS QUEEN IN LOWER SECTIONS)

FRAME WITH COMB

CELLS (HOLD BABY BEES, HONEY, AND POLLEN)

DEEP HIVE BOX

ENTRANCE

LANDING PLATFORM

WE ARE HERE

MEANWHILE

BOB'S BETTER BEES

WATER

COMING FROM THE WEST

The guards smelled our bee spray and our bee food. They let us pass! Other workers took our nectar and bustled off with it.
"Hooray! We're free to explore the hive!" sang out Ms. Frizzle.

The first thing we saw was our bee.
She was doing a strange dance.
Other bees crowded around her,
touching her and listening to her.
Ms. Frizzle said the dance was a "language."
With her dance, the bee "told" others
which way to go to the flowers
she had found.

OUR BEE

MEANWHILE

SNIFF
SNIFF

COMING FROM THE EAST

THE ROUND DANCE
by Phil

This dance tells bees that a food source is close to the hive. The dancing bee walks in a circle, then turns around and goes the other way.

The other bees go outside and fly in a circular pattern near the hive until they find the flowers.

BEE-HIVE

The dance helped the bees find food faster. They did not have to waste time looking for it. They flew off in the direction of the flowers we had visited.

BEES HAVE MANY DANCES.

EACH DANCE "SAYS" SOMETHING DIFFERENT.

DOROTHY ANN'S BIG BOOK OF BEES

New bees gathered around our bee
to get the latest "news."
We passed the dancing bee
and went deeper into the hive.

DOESN'T THE DANCE LANGUAGE OF BEES GIVE YOU A SENSE OF WONDER, ARNOLD?

YES, I WONDER WHICH WAY IS OUT.

THE WAGGLE DANCE
by Carmen
This dance tells bees that a food source is far away. It also tells which way to fly. The dancing bee makes a figure-eight. She waggles her body on the middle line.

① If the bee waggles straight up, the other bees fly toward the sun.

② If the bee waggles to the left, the other bees fly to the left of the sun.

③ If the bee waggles to the right, the other bees fly to the right of the sun.

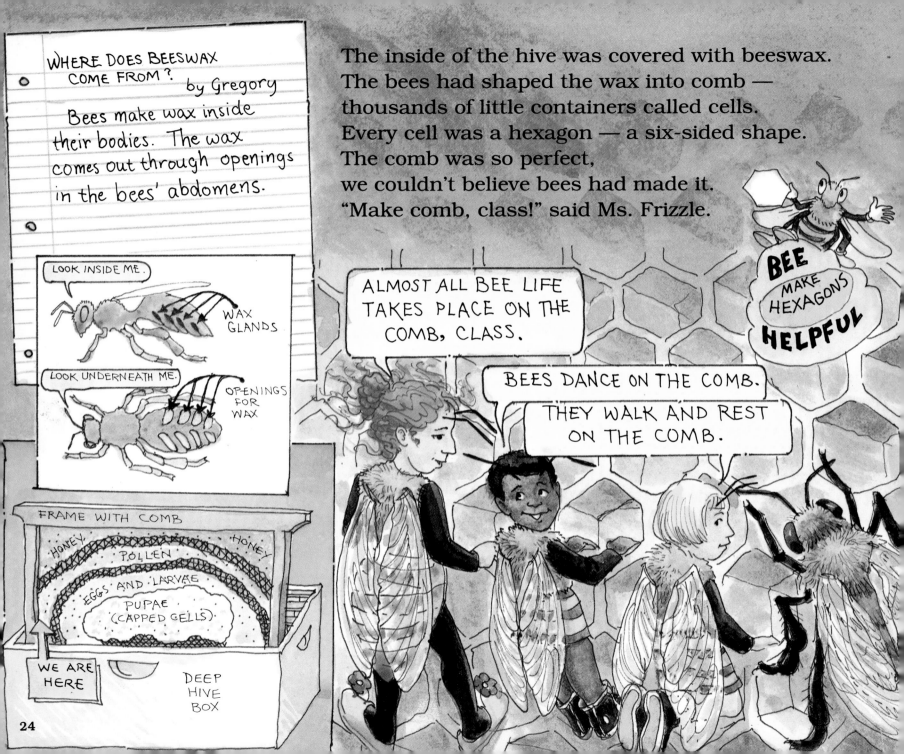

WHERE DOES BEESWAX COME FROM? by Gregory

Bees make wax inside their bodies. The wax comes out through openings in the bees' abdomens.

LOOK INSIDE ME.

WAX GLANDS

LOOK UNDERNEATH ME.

OPENINGS FOR WAX

FRAME WITH COMB

HONEY
HONEY
POLLEN
EGGS AND LARVAE
PUPAE (CAPPED CELLS)

WE ARE HERE

DEEP HIVE BOX

The inside of the hive was covered with beeswax.
The bees had shaped the wax into comb —
thousands of little containers called cells.
Every cell was a hexagon — a six-sided shape.
The comb was so perfect,
we couldn't believe bees had made it.
"Make comb, class!" said Ms. Frizzle.

BEE MAKE HEXAGONS HELPFUL

ALMOST ALL BEE LIFE TAKES PLACE ON THE COMB, CLASS.

BEES DANCE ON THE COMB.

THEY WALK AND REST ON THE COMB.

We did our best, but our cells
came out pretty lopsided.
Luckily, the bees didn't notice us.
They just tore down our cells
and built them over again.
Other bees were busy with other jobs,
such as making honey.

BEES RAISE BABIES
IN THE COMB CELLS.

THEY STORE NECTAR AND
POLLEN IN THE CELLS.

THEY MAKE HONEY
IN THE CELLS, TOO.

THAT'S SWEET
OF THEM.

HOW BEES MAKE COMB
by Rachel

A bee uses her back and
middle legs to pass wax
to her front legs.
Then she chews and shapes
the wax into cells.

Honey bees make the
comb cells tilt up
so the honey doesn't
drip out!

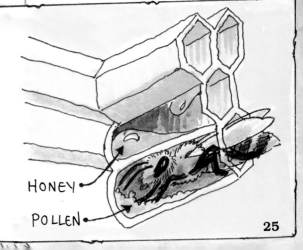

HONEY

POLLEN

25

We saw the bees changing nectar into honey.
First, they added chemicals
from glands inside their heads.
The chemicals changed the
nectar-sugars into honey-sugars.
Then they spread droplets out
and fanned them with their wings.
This dried up most of the water —
leaving the honey thick, sticky,
and extra-sweet.
We fanned, too, and helped make honey.

26

Ms. Frizzle said it was okay to eat some honey, as long as we left plenty for the bees.
"They need a good supply of honey to help them survive over the winter," she explained.

IT'S COZY IN A BEEHIVE.

IT'S TASTY IN A BEEHIVE.

IT'S EASY TO HELP WITH THIS JOB!

HONEY IS GOOD FOOD!
by Molly
Honey is a very good food for bees, humans, and other animals. But human babies under one year should not eat raw honey.

YOU'RE NOT OLD ENOUGH FOR HONEY, HONEY.

HONEY

BEE EAT HONEY!

HAPPY

27

We stopped eating honey long enough
to notice a bunch of worker bees nearby.
They were tending a larger bee
with a long thin body.
She was the queen bee!
As the queen walked from cell to cell,
she laid a small white egg in each one.

The workers touched the queen with their antennae,
they licked her with their tongues,
and they fed her by mouth-to-mouth exchange.

BE A BEE!
TEND THE QUEEN!

WE CAN TOUCH HER
WITH OUR ANTENNAE.

WE CAN GIVE
HER SOME
HONEY.

LET'S JUST SKIP
THE MOUTH-TO-
MOUTH PART.

GOOD IDEA.

29

WHY DOES A LARVA EAT A LOT?
SO THE PUPA CAN CHANGE A LOT!
by Arnold

Pupae do not eat. So where do they get the energy to grow the parts of adult bees?

They use the fat and tissue they stored up when they were larvae.

ANOTHER WORD FROM DOROTHY ANN

Metamorphosis comes from a word that means "change."

"When it is big enough, the larva stops eating," said the Friz. "It spins a silk cocoon around itself. Now it is called a pupa.
The nurse bees put a wax top on the cell.
Inside, the pupa doesn't eat or grow bigger.
It changes into an adult bee.
This is called metamorphosis.

"When the pupae have finished
changing into adult bees,
they chew their way out of their cells,"
continued Ms. Frizzle.
We saw new worker bees emerging.
They let the air dry them off
and started working right away.
Meanwhile, we heard excited buzzing.
What was happening?

BEE GROW UP! ADULT

NOW THE METAMORPHOSIS IS COMPLETE, CHILDREN.

THE BEES ARE ALL GROWN UP.

I'M SO PROUD OF THEM.

THE ROAD FROM **EGG** TO **BEE**

EGG   LARVA   PUPA   ADULT

The queen was leaving the hive!
And she was taking almost half
the workers with her!
They flew away in a thick swarm.
What would become of the hive now?

34

Ms. Frizzle led the way to the queen cells. Two new queens emerged at the same time.

After they had dried out, they had a terrible fight. One queen stung the other queen to death!

Then she killed the other queen pupae in their cells. Now she was the new queen.

TWO QUEENS? I THOUGHT...

THERE WAS ONLY...

ONE QUEEN IN A HIVE.

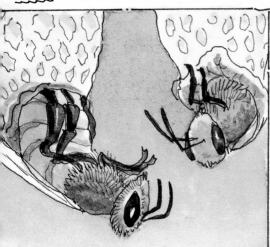

A QUEEN BEE CAN STING MANY TIMES   by Arnold

Unlike worker bees, which can sting only once, the queen bee can pull her stinger out of the victim and sting again.

YOU WERE ABSOLUTELY RIGHT.

THE STRONGER QUEEN SURVIVES TO PASS ON HER STRENGTH TO HER CHILDREN.

QUEENS MEET DRONES
by Wanda
Thousands of drones from many colonies gather in one place.
When queens are ready to mate, they fly there, too.
Usually drones do not mate with the queen from their own colony.

ANOTHER WORD FROM DOROTHY ANN
Nuptial comes from a word that means "Wedding."

Drones

New Queen

The worker bees pushed the new queen out of the hive.
Ms. Frizzle said she was going on a nuptial flight — a flight to mate with drones.

AFTER THE NEW QUEEN MATES, SHE'LL RETURN TO THE HIVE AND START LAYING EGGS.

HER EGGS WILL HATCH AND REPLACE THE WORKERS THAT LEFT WITH THE OLD QUEEN.

THEN THE HIVE WILL BE AS STRONG AS IT WAS BEFORE.

MAYBE YES, MAYBE NO...

After the new queen left,
we heard heavy footsteps.
It was a bear, trying to steal the honey
and the bee larvae!
The workers flew out and tried to sting the bear,
but its thick fur protected its body.

MEANWHILE

BEEKEEPER STILL ON THE WAY

IF THE BEAR BREAKS OPEN THE HIVE...

AND EATS ALL THE HONEY AND THE LARVAE...

THE BEES MAY NOT SURVIVE!

WE HAVE TO HELP!

STING HIM!

I CAN'T GET THROUGH!

HELP!

COMMON HIVE RAIDERS
by Tim

Skunks →

Bears →

← Wasps

Bees from other hives →

Bees can defeat most robbers, but bears are hard to beat.

BEWARE

NEVER GET CLOSE TO BEARS. THEY MAY LOOK CUTE, BUT THEY ARE VERY DANGEROUS.

We flew out and dived at the bear, but it kept coming at the hive. "We have to use strategy, class," called the Friz. "We'll lure the bear away!"

BEE FOR ANYTHING PREPARE

BE A BEE! DEFEND THE HIVE!

BUT I DON'T WANT TO HURT A CUTE LITTLE BEAR.

I WOULDN'T SAY CUTE AND LITTLE.

I'D SAY BIG AND HUNGRY!

Ms. Frizzle made a beeline for the beehive-bus —
and we followed.
The jar of honey that had spilled before was
still on the floor.
The bear smelled the honey and came after us.
"Ms. Frizzle!" we yelled. "Do something!"
She stepped on the gas, and the bus lurched forward.

39

As we rounded a corner,
the honey jar rolled out the bus door.
As the jar fell, it returned to its normal size.
The bear started eating honey and forgot all about us.

40

Ms. Frizzle reached for a joystick
on the dashboard.
To our relief, the bus lifted off.
It wasn't a beehive-bus anymore. It was a bee-bus!
Down below, we saw the new queen returning home
from her nuptial flight.

THE HIVE IS SAFE!

WE'RE SAFE!

WE'LL MEET THE BEEKEEPER
ANOTHER DAY, CLASS. RIGHT
NOW, WE'RE RETURNING TO
THE CLASSROOM.

IT'S ABOUT TIME.

We returned home from our flight, too.
The instant its six feet touched the ground
in the school parking lot, the bee-bus changed.

It was a full-size school bus again.
We were human kids again.

45

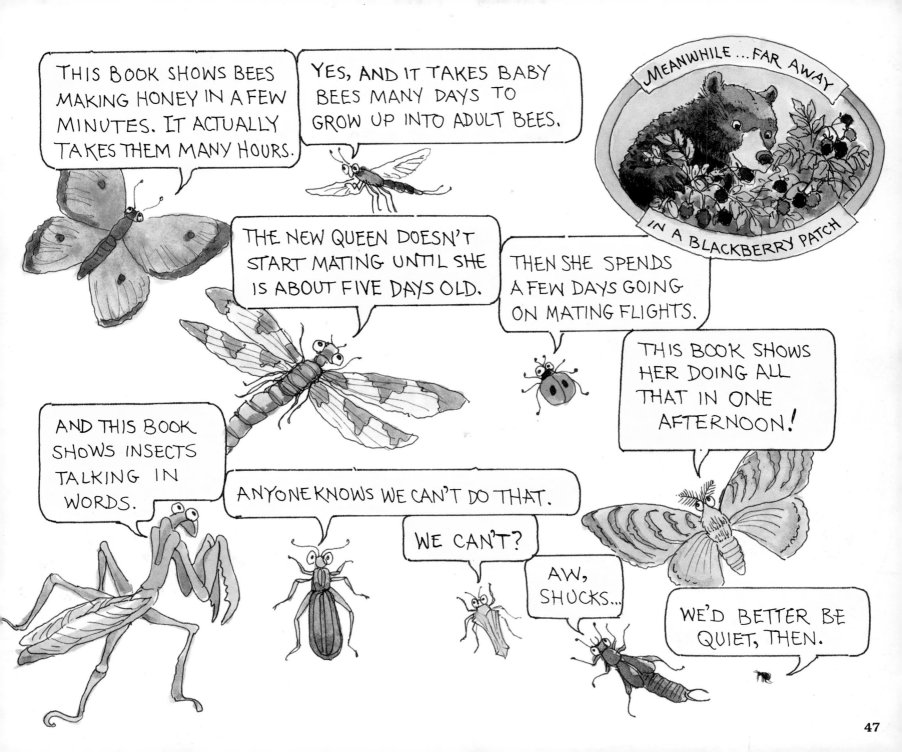

47

LADYBIRD BOOKS, INC.
Auburn, Maine 04210 U.S.A.
© LADYBIRD BOOKS LTD 1988
Loughborough, Leicestershire, England

Printed in England

The Christmas Robin

Adapted by David Hately from
The Wise Robin by Noel Barr
Illustrated by Peter Stevenson

Ladybird Books

It was cold, very cold, and snow lay thick on the ground. Mr. Robin searched in vain for food. He couldn't find any insects to eat, because they were hiding away from the cold. He couldn't dig for worms, because the ground was too hard and icy.

At last, cold and hungry, he gave up and flew back to his nest.

Mrs. Robin was hungry, too. ''Is there anything for supper?'' she asked.

Mr. Robin shook his head. He tried to say ''No,'' but it came out as ''Brrr.''

''Never mind,'' said Mrs. Robin cheerfully. ''Perhaps we'll have better luck tomorrow.''

But the next day was even colder, and still Mr. Robin could find nothing to eat.

Mr. Robin decided to search for food in the garden of a nearby house. Suddenly there was a noise from the house. With a tweet of alarm, Mr. Robin hid behind a snowman.

Peeking around, he saw a window being opened. A hand scattered something on the window sill.

When everything was quiet again, Mr. Robin flew up to the window to investigate.

Perching on the window sill, Mr. Robin saw some neat little holes in the snow. He stuck his beak down one of the holes and could hardly believe his luck when he found a juicy raisin.

Besides raisins, there were crumbs of bread and cake. There was even some cinnamon toast!

Mr. Robin hurried back to Mrs. Robin, and together they returned to the window sill, where they enjoyed a delicious supper.

When they were finished, Mrs. Robin peered in through the window, twisting her head this way and that to get a better view.

Suddenly she gasped. "Look!" she said. "There's a fir tree growing inside this house!"

The Robins had never seen a tree like it. At the top was a bright star, and hanging from the branches were twinkling lights, shiny colored glass balls, little toys, and candy canes.

There were also some long pieces of glittering tinsel.

"Look at that silver moss!" breathed Mrs. Robin. "Isn't it beautiful?"

Later that evening, when they were back in their nest, Mrs. Robin said, ''Wouldn't our nest look lovely with some of that silver moss woven in among the twigs? Will you get some for me, dear?''

Mr. Robin gulped. He was afraid that if he went into the house he might get caught. But he couldn't bear to disappoint Mrs. Robin. ''Of course I will. I'll get some for you tomorrow,'' he said, trying to sound brave. ''Now let's get some sleep.''

The next morning, Mr. Robin flew over to the window sill. There was no one in the room, and the window was open. He fluttered in and settled on a branch of the tree.

Suddenly the door burst open and into the room came
two large people and two small ones.

"Merry Christmas, Matthew and Emily!" said the two large people. "Choose a present from the Christmas tree."

Mr. Robin shivered with fright and tried to hide.

The little person called Matthew asked for a candy cane. But the one called Emily pointed to Mr. Robin and cried, "I want the toy robin!"

"But I'm not a toy!" thought Mr. Robin. "I'm a real, live robin!" And just as a big hand reached up to lift him from the tree, he sprang to the top branch, threw back his head, and started to sing at the top of his voice. As he trilled and whistled and chirped, the people clapped their hands.

When he had finished his song, Mr. Robin flew out the window and hopped down onto the window sill.

Emily ran across the room. ''Thank you, little robin,'' she said, ''for making this the best Christmas tree ever. Come and see us again!''

When Mrs. Robin heard what had happened, she forgot all about the tinsel. ''As long as you're safe,'' she said, ''that's all that matters.''

But twelve days after his adventure, Mr. Robin found
the fir tree lying near the trash cans. Caught on its
branches were some scraps of tinsel.

Mr. Robin took them back to decorate the nest.
Mrs. Robin was overjoyed. She had her silver moss
after all!